Whisker Wizard

Random House 🏠 New York

Copyright © 2021 by Jennifer Holm and Matthew Holm

All rights reserved. Published in the United States by Random House Children's Books, a division of Penguin Random House LLC, New York.

Random House and the colophon are registered trademarks of Penguin Random House LLC.

Visit us on the Web! rhcbooks.com

Educators and librarians, for a variety of teaching tools, visit us at RHTeachersLibrarians.com

Library of Congress Cataloging-in-Publication Data
Names: Holm, Jennifer L., author. | Holm, Matthew, illustrator.
Title: Whisker Wizard / Jennifer L. Holm & Matthew Holm.
Description: First edition. | New York: Random House Children's Books, [2021] |
Series: Babymouse tales from the locker; 5
Summary: "Babymouse becomes an influencer after she tries out a new whisker style and posts a tutorial online." —Provided by publisher.
Identifiers: LCCN 2020037423 | ISBN 978-0-593-11939-6 (hardback) | ISBN 978-0-593-11940-2 (glb) | ISBN 978-0-593-11941-9 (ebook)
Subjects: CYAC: Fame—Fiction. | Popularity—Fiction. | Social media—Fiction. | Middle schools—Fiction. | Schools—Fiction. | Mice—Fiction. Animals—Fiction. | Humorous stories.
Classification: LCC PZ7.H732226 Whi 2021 | DDC [Fic]—dc23

Printed in the United States of America
10 9 8 7 6 5 4 3 2 1
First Edition

**For our amazing
whisker wizard of an editor:
Diane!**

Contents

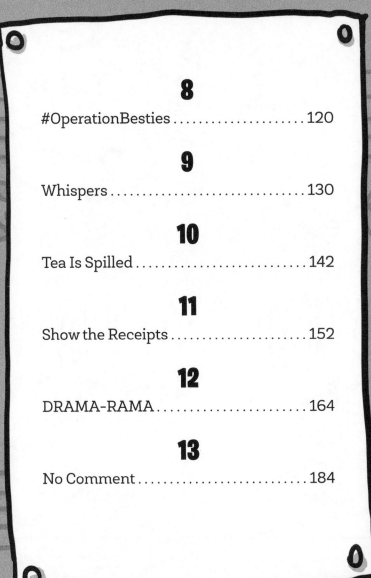

Bored

It had been a long week of school. Finally, the weekend had arrived, and I had plans.

Big plans.

BABYMOUSE, ARE YOU ENJOYING THIS BEAUTIFUL WEATHER?

YEP!

I heard footsteps in the hallway.

"Babymouse," my mom called. "It's a beautiful day outside. Why don't you get up and have a little exercise?"

Ugh. I grumbled, "How nice a day could it really even be?"

My mom came into my room and drew

my curtains. I shielded my eyes from the bright sunlight.

"See for yourself!" she chirped.

"Okay, okay, I'll get up," I promised. "Just please, no more light!"

"No problem," Mom replied. "But if you're not out of that bed in ten minutes, I'm sending in Squeak."

"Anything but that!" I replied, shooting straight up in mock horror.

My mom laughed on her way out of the room.

Of course, I closed the curtains and immediately went back to watching my nature cam. The squirrels were adorable.

☆ ♡ ☆

Ten minutes later (almost on the dot—how does she **do** that?), my little brother, Squeak, poked his head into my room. He was eating a lollipop, and he had it all over his face and smeared on his hands.

I pretended not to notice him, but he didn't seem to care.

"Mom wants you to get up and get dressed, Babymouse," he said, playing with my cell phone. "She said I could touch all your stuff until you got out of bed."

Argh!

Time to start the day.

☆ ♥ ☆

After kicking Squeak out, I brushed my teeth and put on a fresh outfit.

Then I climbed back into bed and started watching clips of Fabi at the Fabulous Film Awards on my tablet. Fabi is my favorite actress. She's so famous she only has one name!

Fabi had starred in an old-timey black-and-white film recently, so I typed "black and white" into my browser. But that just led me down a rabbit hole of panda videos. I laughed as I watched cubs cuddle, tumble down hills, and fall asleep eating bamboo.

My dad knocked on the door. Now it was his turn to pester me.

"Babymouse," he said. "Why don't you come spend some time with your family?"

He put a pile of clean laundry on the floor by my closet.

"If laundry is the most exciting thing going on out there, I think I'm all good," I replied.

"But don't you want to come down and see what's going on in the world?"

"I can see everything worth seeing from right here," I told him, pointing to my tablet screen.

Just being cute!

BABY PANDA CHANNEL

"Well, you know where to find us if you run out of videos to watch," he said. He left, pulling the door closed behind him.

That was ridiculous, I thought. It would be impossible to watch all the videos in the world. Didn't he know more were being uploaded all the time?!

But the truth was that I was bored.

EVERYTHING IS SO BORING!

MAYBE GO OUTSIDE AND GET SOME FRESH AIR?

THAT'S EVEN **MORE** BORING!

Instead, I started watching infomercials.

I lazily scrolled down my screen. Just then, something caught my eye: a do-it-yourself whisker formula.

Now, I had been using Basic Whiskers for as long as I could remember. Just like my mom, and her mom, and probably her mom before that.

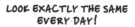

BASIC WHISKERS

LOOK EXACTLY THE SAME EVERY DAY!

ALL-IN-ONE. PARABEN-FREE.
SULFATE-FREE. ACID-FREE.
FRAGRANCE-FREE. RESULTS-FREE.
HYPOALLERGENIC.
DERMATOLOGIST-RECOMMENDED.

I had been trying to convince my mom to buy something new and exciting for our whiskers, but she wouldn't budge.

"Why be special when you can be **basic**?" she always replied, quoting the commercial.

She insisted on using the same product, year after year.

Even the packaging looked a hundred years old.

Still, even though Mom wouldn't **buy** anything new, she never said I couldn't make my own whisker formula from a recipe. And if the recipe was on the internet, it had to be legit, right?

I looked more closely at the description. It was very intriguing.

Now, that sounded awesome! Besides, all those ingredients sounded safe-ish. Most of them we had in our kitchen cabinets. I decided to give it a try.

I jumped out of bed and ran downstairs.

"Coming to help?" Dad exclaimed as I ran by. He and Mom were still folding clothes in the living room.

"Sorry! Busy!" I said. I had whisker serum to make!

First, I needed to gather the ingredients, which was a lot harder than I had expected. It was Saturday, and grocery-shopping day was Sunday, so the pantry was pretty bare. There was a lot of oatmeal (what was it with parents and oatmeal?) and a half-finished box of stale granola. I also discovered several cans of soup that nobody liked, mostly cream of mushroom and split pea. There was no way split pea soup should go in anything, so I gave up on the pantry and looked around.

But I finally found a real lemon in the produce drawer, hidden behind a bag of yucky-looking parsley.

On to the mustard! I opened the refrigerator and looked inside.

I checked the recipe, but it didn't specify which type to use. Perplexed, I took a little of each, just to be safe.

Plop!

Into the mixing bowl went all the mustards.

I had the same problem with the vinegar. I opened a cabinet and saw all different types: distilled white vinegar, red vinegar, rice vinegar, apple cider vinegar, balsamic vinegar, and malt vinegar. I could only reach one of them, or it would have been hard to choose. (It was distilled white vinegar, in case you were wondering.)

Finally, I was almost done. The last item was going to be easy: mayonnaise. I knew that my dad had just bought some.

I searched the fridge, but the bottle wasn't where it usually was.

Hmm. I looked around the kitchen without any success.

"Dad!" I called. "Do you know where the mayo is?"

"In here!" Squeak replied from the dining room.

I hurried into the dining room, where Squeak was surrounded by mutilated plastic lemons. I was just in time to see him squeeze the last of the mayo onto his sandwich.

"NoOoOo!" I yelled, scrabbling toward him.

It was almost in slow motion, as I saw my chance to make the serum slip away onto a disgusting mess of peanut butter and potato chips.

I took the bottle from him and did my best to squeeze more out, but it wasn't going to be easy.

It didn't work, so I applied more pressure.

Soon, I had rigged up a contraption consisting of a giant encyclopedia, my mom's hand weights, and a bowling ball to try to get the last drops of mayo out.

MAN, THAT'S A WHOLE LOT OF WORK FOR WHISKER CARE!

No luck!

I went back to see if I could get some from Squeak's sandwich, but he was just finishing his last bite.

He showed me how it was all over his face and fingers.

Yuck! I gagged, avoiding him.

But I wasn't giving up yet. All I needed to do was find a mayo-like substance somewhere in the kitchen.

I looked through the refrigerator. There were dozens of jars, bottles, and tubes full of condiments. Lots of them were too hard to open, a bunch were super smelly, and one was even expired!

(At least, it smelled expired. It was labeled "Sour Cream." Why would anyone buy cream that was already sour? It didn't make sense!)

But on I went, narrowing down my options. The finalists on my list were vanilla yogurt, French onion dip, ranch dressing, anchovy paste, and horseradish.

Decisions, decisions.

I picked up the horseradish bottle. It looked old. Really old. In fact, the label on the back was so faded that I couldn't read the ingredients. I guess that should have been a sign it was expired and I shouldn't use it. But I **did** like horses an awful lot. And from what I could remember, they usually had smooth, sleek hair. So I decided to go with that.

I dumped the horseradish into the bowl with the other ingredients. Man, I'd thought the anchovy paste smelled bad. The horse-radish was even worse!

When all the ingredients were mixed together, the concoction reminded me of a bubbling swamp. Not a good thing. But I had already spent over an hour making the recipe, so I couldn't stop now!

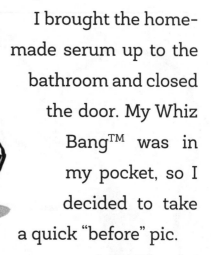

I brought the home-made serum up to the bathroom and closed the door. My Whiz Bang™ was in my pocket, so I decided to take a quick "before" pic.

"Here goes nothing!" I said to no one in particular.

I carefully applied a large portion of the gloop to my whiskers.

I set my Whiz Bang™ timer for three minutes, as instructed by the recipe.

The smell was so terrible that I gagged a little. My eyes burned like I was cutting into an onion. But I soon forgot all about my eyes stinging because my whiskers started burning, too!

(Maybe that's why they put the warning label under the recipe?)

I tried to hold my breath as I waited. Finally, the timer reached 0:00.

Beep! Beep! Beep!

I had never been so happy to hear an alarm go off in my entire life!

I scrubbed the mess off my face as quickly as I could.

As soon as I'd washed it all off, I stared in the mirror. My face looked different, all right, but that was mostly because my cheeks were bright red and swollen.

Despite that, I attempted to style my whiskers. I decided to get creative, twisting them around and around until they stayed put.

Finally, I came up with an interesting style. I snapped a selfie, my "after," so I could send two pics to my friends.

I logged on to my group chat with Penny, Georgie, Wilson, and Duckie to see what they thought of my new look.

check out my new look!

☺

Fancy!

. . . ?

wut do you call it?

um . . . the Twist?!

I was glad Penny liked my look, but I had very little time to chat, because I suddenly heard a scream downstairs.

"Babymouse!" my mom yelled. "Come down here this instant!"

I gulped, remembering the huge mess I had made in the kitchen.

"Coming!" I yelled back.

A minute later, I was in the pantry getting cleaning supplies. After tripping over the broom and mop, I reached up to the top shelf to grab the paper towels.

That's when I saw it.

Twist

I spent the next two hours cleaning the kitchen and vacuuming fake-lemon bits out of the dining room rug.

Then I got a text from Penny.

Can I post ur selfie to WHISKER WIZARDS? It's a hot new style website.

Sure, y not?

Cool! Thx.

Penny sent me a link. I put away the vacuum and ran upstairs. I logged on to my computer and clicked on the website.

The site was pretty cool! In no time, I got totally sucked in, and I spent the rest of the day checking out new looks. The hours ticked by, and I got sleepier and sleepier. But I couldn't tear myself away from the screen. In the end, I fell asleep with my finger on the scroll button. Now, that's dedication!

☆ ♥ ☆

By the time Monday morning rolled around, my face felt better. Just for fun, I decided to wear my whiskers to school in the Twist.

While I was checking out my whiskers in the locker mirror, I saw Felicia Furrypaws and two of her friends in the reflection. Then I noticed the oddest thing: they had their whiskers styled the same way as I did!

I couldn't believe it! Felicia Furrypaws! The most popular girl in school! Was I still dreaming? Had I accidentally been transported into another universe where I was actually ahead of a trend—or had maybe even **started** a trend?? Or, more likely, were they just making fun of me somehow?

The weirdness didn't stop there.

All day, I saw other kids with the same whisker style as me. In fact, kids in every grade seemed to be rocking my look.

Just when I thought things couldn't get any weirder, I saw our school custodian wearing the Twist!

My head was spinning. Was it all just a coincidence? Or had someone stolen my idea?

Maybe I should have trademarked my whisker style, I thought.

After school, I took the bus home, as usual. On the way, my Whiz Bang™ buzzed. It was a message from Penny.

My insides were bursting with excitement, but I tried to keep calm. I didn't want everyone to know how thrilled I was to be cool. Caring about being cool is, of course, very **uncool.**

When I walked into the house, Mom was in the kitchen, making cupcakes with Squeak.

"Has anyone seen the whisk—" she said, stopping short when she saw me.

"Whiskers!" Squeak finished, pointing at me.

"Wow," she commented. "I like your new look, Babymouse."

"Just trying out a different style," I said.

"Neat," Mom said. "Very creative."

"Thanks!" I replied.

Mom found the whisk and began to beat the batter. I couldn't wait for cupcakes!

☆ ♥ ☆

That night, after dinner, we sat in the living room to watch TV. Dad brought in the tray of cupcakes and put one down in front of me.

"So, does this new look have anything to do with the smelly concoction I found in the bathroom this morning?"

"Oops, sorry!" I replied, taking off the cupcake wrapper. "I'll clean it up before I go to bed."

Dad smiled. "Sounds good," he said.

He sat next to me and turned on the news channel. On the screen, the shot cut to a reporter.

Both my cupcake and my jaw fell to the floor with a **clunk**.

"That's funny," Dad said, pointing. "Look at that reporter's whiskers."

"She has the same style as you, Babymouse!" Mom exclaimed.

Tutorial

I expected that everything would soon go back to normal, but when I arrived at school, a small crowd was gathered around my locker.

Had I left a stinky sandwich in there the day before?

But when I approached, people actually seemed **happy** to see me.

"There she is!" someone cried.

I double-checked to make sure Felicia wasn't standing behind me. But sure enough, they were talking about **me.**

"You're Babymouse, right?" a boy asked.

"Yeah, um, hi," I said nervously. I couldn't help but notice they all had their whiskers in the Twist.

They looked like they had tried to do the Twist, but it hadn't worked out so well.

In fact, on Whisker Wizards, I would classify most of them as #TwistFails.

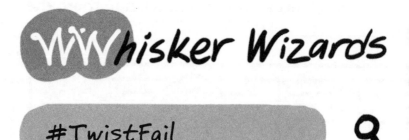

"We need you!" one of the girls said, tugging on my arm. "You have to tell us how to do your look!"

"Yeah," another girl said. "I tried a ton of different things yesterday, and nothing worked."

It was incredible! No one ever wanted my advice on anything.

I looked up to see Penny down the hall, speed-walking past the hall monitor.

"Babymouse!" she gushed. "Everyone is talking about you. Did you see the reporter on the news last night? Your Twist has gone viral!"

"Please, you have to tell us how to do the Twist!" the first girl pleaded.

I looked at Penny, who nodded approvingly.

"Give the people what they want," she encouraged.

"Uh, well," I began, "I found this recipe for a whisker serum online."

"Where?" the second girl asked.

"And what was in it?" asked another, tapping me on the shoulder.

I was starting to get overwhelmed. There was so much to explain, and so little time.

As if Penny had read my mind, she pulled me through the crowd to my locker.

"Check out Whisker Wizards tonight," she told everyone. "Babymouse will post a tutorial explaining exactly how she does her famous Twist."

"Will you really, Babymouse?" a voice asked.

I nodded.

The warning bell rang, and the crowd scattered. As everyone walked away, I heard "Yay!" and "Hooray!" mixed with one "Eh, I thought it looked better online."

"Talk later, Babymouse," said Penny, giving me a thumbs-up.

Stunned, I struggled to open my locker. It took me several tries. Finally, it clicked open just before the final bell sounded.

Ring!

I watched a flurry of papers float to the hallway floor and tried to process what had just happened. Then it started to dawn on me what was going on.

People wanted **my** opinion.

People were actually looking up to **me**!

The day had taken an interesting turn. (Get it, Twist joke?!)

Less excitingly, I was late for homeroom. Typical.

☆ ♥ ☆

Students came up to me during the day to ask about my whisker look. I gave them as many tips and tricks as I could. Everyone listened intently. Some even took notes!

In health class, someone passed me a note. I passed it down the line, as usual. But then something weird happened: the kid next to me passed it **back.**

Was this what it felt like to be popular? I was so excited, I wasn't even worried about getting in trouble.

In fact, I wanted everyone to know. I tried to cough and sneeze a lot to subtly call attention to myself, but the teacher just sent me to the nurse.

It happened again in science class, and then in math.

I even thought someone was passing me a note during gym class, but it was just the baton for a relay race. Oops!

By lunch, I was completely exhausted from explaining the Twist so many times.

I couldn't wait to get home and try to make the tutorial. I ran from the bus to my house, bounded up the stairs, and closed my bedroom door.

I was ready!

Until I realized . . . I didn't **exactly** know what a tutorial was.

do u really think I should do a tutorial?

Yes, you have to!

ok, kewl. just 1 question.

?

wuts a tutorial?

lol I'll call u

Penny called me right away, and I picked up on the first ring.

"You just take a video of yourself explaining how to do something, and you post it on the internet," she said.

"Got it!" I replied. "That sounds easy."

"It is," she said. "I watch them all the time. I'll send you some links. I'd come over and help you, but I have too much homework tonight."

"No worries," I replied.

As soon as I hung up with Penny, she sent me a bunch of tutorials.

Tutorial: How to apply whisker mascara

Tutorial: Get that mane under control!

I watched all the videos. Each one made it seem so easy! There was even a tutorial by a five-year-old on how to braid whiskers.

Anyone can do this, I thought. **I can do this!**

I wrote myself a script, got all the ingredients ready, and set up my camera.

That's when I realized that filming was going to be harder than I'd thought.

To start off, I couldn't hold the phone because I needed both hands to style my whiskers in the tutorial.

(Believe me, I tried lots of alternatives.)

I tried propping my phone up in different spots in my room. But every time I started to get the hang of filming, it would fall over, or only half of my face would be in the image, or my voice would sound muffled and far away.

It soon became clear I would have to bring in outside help.

There was only one thing for me to do: I would have to ask Squeak to be my videographer.

☆ ♥ ☆

I found him downstairs in the living room, watching cartoons. In exchange for his name in the credits and a week of me doing his chores, Squeak agreed to record the tutorial for me.

But it didn't end there. He printed a professional videography contract and made me sign it right in front of him! He even added a clause that said I had to give him a pack of gum for every take, and two packs of gum for every take more than five.

"Gum overtime," he explained to me. "Industry standard."

I shook my head. The whole thing was ridiculous, but what choice did I have? I couldn't show my (perfectly whiskered) face in school tomorrow without having posted the tutorial tonight. Everyone would be so let down.

I reached into my backpack and pulled out three sticks of gum.

"You'll get the rest of the pack when the job is done," I told him.

He nodded and popped all three into his mouth.

☆ ♡ ☆

I'll tell you one thing: Penny was wrong about tutorials being easy. There were so many things to do at once, and Squeak wasn't making it easier by putting the pressure on.

The first take ended up sounding kind of like, well, this:

HI, MY NAME IS BABYMOUSE, AND TODAY I'M GOING TO TELL YOU ABOUT HOW MY NAME IS BABYMOUSE. I MEAN HOW TO TWIST YOUR BABYMOUSE, AND TODAY IS GOING TO TELL YOU ABOUT MY NAME IS WHISKERS. NO, I MEAN YOUR NAME IS BABYMOUSE, AND TODAY YOU'RE GOING TO TELL ME ABOUT WHISKERING YOUR TWISTERS.

#Facepalm

The second time, I looked in the wrong places entirely!

So much time passed that the sun started to go down. My room got too dark, so we had to add more lights.

What a headache! And this didn't even include perfecting the demonstration itself!

It was so simple to create my Twists when I was just having fun and playing around. But now that people were depending on me and there was a time limit—not to mention a slowly disappearing bubble gum budget—everything was so much harder.

My hands shook as I tried to create the perfect spiral over and over again.

Most times, one side would come out looking good, and then the other side would be a total disaster.

Sometimes, I thought I'd fit in better at a haunted house than a beauty salon.

THE HORROR!

I ended up having to record the whole thing about nine times.

But finally, I completed a near-perfect take. It was a whisker miracle! I didn't flub my lines even once, and my whiskers came out really well!

I grabbed my Whiz Bang™ from Squeak so I could play the recording back. I searched the videos on my phone, but the last one was just a video of Squeak with my voice floating in the background.

My stomach dropped.

"Oh no!" I yelled, realizing what had happened. "Did you have the camera set to selfie mode during that whole video?"

Squeak shrugged.

"Technical difficulties," he said. "Call my agent."

He took the open pack of gum from my backpack and walked off.

Typical.

In the end, I had to cut and paste a bunch of different videos together to make a tutorial I could actually post. It came out kind of weird, but at least my whiskers looked good!

Finally, I posted the video on Whisker Wizards. Now all I could do was wait. . . .

Luv U!!!!

My tutorial had finally gone live on Whisker Wizards. I couldn't believe how exciting it was to have my whiskers out there!

One thing I had noticed on all the videos was how many "luvs" and comments each one got.

The more people who viewed your videos, the more popular you became online. I was really hoping to get a big following ASAP.

As I waited for more views and followers, I realized I could get the ball rolling by watching the video myself as many times as possible. (I guess that makes me my own biggest fan!)

I then sent the video to the girls who'd mobbed me that morning. When I had gotten up to twenty-one views (nineteen from me and two from randoms), I decided it was time to go to bed.

After what seemed like forever, I finally fell asleep.

Of course, I dreamed all night about being a famous tutorialist. Paparazzi took pictures of me, reporters stood outside my house with camera crews, and my fans chased me down the street.

☆ ♡ ☆

In the morning, I woke up late and had to rush off to school without even checking my video stats.

Not surprisingly, school was just like the day before.

Everyone crowded around my locker,

commenting on the Whisker Wizards video and asking me for advice.

"We loved your tutorial, Babymouse!" said the girl who passed me the note the day before.

"Yeah, I watched it three times in a row," said another. "Check out my whiskers!" She plucked at one of her whiskers, and it sprang perfectly back into place. **Boing!**

"The only weird thing," said a boy from my homeroom, "was that chewing and popping sound in the background the whole time. . . ."

SQUEAK! I thought. But I kept my teeth clenched in a smile.

"Anyway, can't wait to see what you do next," he continued.

Me neither, I thought.

I couldn't concentrate at school. I was trying to think of ideas for a new video tutorial, but coming up empty.

The more I tried to think, the more my mind went blank. Of course, that made it even harder to brainstorm ideas. What if this was it for me? What if I never had another creative idea for as long as I lived? Would I become a washed-up has-been, hopelessly living in the past?

I couldn't let that happen, so I finally began to brainstorm new styles.

During math class, I tried to think of what "protractor" whiskers would look like.

In science, I daydreamed about an "amoeba" style.

Gym class had me wondering about a "dirty sneaker" look.

I was scribbling in my notebook so much that my teachers actually complimented me on my "newfound love of learning." Little did they know it was just ideas for my new vlog!

SCRIBBLE
SCRIBBLE

Protractor? whiskers.

50°

Amoeba whiskers?

dirty sneaker whiskers?

(ew!)

I got home and dumped my backpack out onto the floor of my room. I picked up my notebook and flipped through the pages.

Surely, I had come up with something good after thinking nonstop for a whole day.

Maybe I could do a variation of the Twist? I got out a notepad and jotted down ideas.

The DNA strand

The spiral staircase

ARGH.

All the looks were basically the same. Was I a one-whisker wonder?

I got up and began to pace around my room.

"Ouch!" I exclaimed.

I had stepped on something sharp. I looked down to see a metal paper clip.

Hmm. Now, **that** was an interesting shape.

What if I could make my whiskers look like a paper clip? I wondered.

Without any better ideas, I decided to try it out.

I played around with my whiskers until I had a look that kind of, sort of, **maybe** resembled a paper clip. And, to my surprise, it actually looked . . . awesome!

I immediately began working on a video! After enlisting Squeak's help—he told me his rate had gone up to **two** packs of gum per take—I was ready to go. (After I made sure the camera wasn't on selfie mode, of course!)

A couple of hours later, my whiskers were on point, and the video was ready to be released to the entire World Wide Web! (Or at least my five subscribers. . . .)

I uploaded it, shot a quick FYI text to Penny, and tumbled into bed, exhausted.

This time, I had no trouble falling asleep.

ZZZZZZZZ...

When I woke up in the morning, I had 104 subscribers!

That got me motivated! If I could get to 100 subscribers, maybe I could get to 1,000, and then 10,000, and then 100,000, and maybe even 1,000,000! I had always been convinced I was destined to be famous. Maybe this was my big break!

Now that I had a new goal—kind of the same one I'd always had, becoming rich and famous—I decided to repeat the same process every day.

My new schedule went like this:*

1) Go to school.
2) Give whisker advice to adoring fans.
3) Come up with new ideas for tutorials.
4) Stop at store for gum on way home.
5) Prepare for video.
6) Record video.
7) Upload video.
8) Enjoy fame.
9) Fall asleep.
10) Do the same thing again the next day.

*I also ate, brushed my teeth, and went to the bathroom at some points during the day, in case you were wondering. But these are unimportant things in the life of an internet celebrity.

I must admit my teachers were not exactly thrilled that I hadn't done any homework in a week, and were threatening to give me detention. But instead of worrying about that and kick-starting my work again, I only thought about what "detention whiskers" might look like, and whether they would go viral.

This wasn't the only obstacle I had to overcome. Slowly, my parents were starting to notice all the missing ingredients from their pantry.

I was going through three jars of mayonnaise a week. (I told Dad I was really into egg salad so he wouldn't be too suspicious.)

Coming up with different looks and doing a new tutorial every day was really wearing me out. It had been so much fun in the beginning, but now it was feeling like real **work**.

(Not to mention that I pretty much owed Squeak an entire gum factory!)

But still, I made tutorial after tutorial.

I came up with the "heart-shaped" whisker style.

The "bow tie" whisker style.

The "swirl" whisker style.

My fan base was still growing, but not as quickly. After each upload, I watched for the number of views and read all the comments. It was like an obsession. Most of the comments were really nice, but there were some mean ones, too, and they stuck out to me the most.

It drove me crazy! I might get "I luv you!" like thirty times in a row, and then "Meh, her whiskers are basic" once—and that was all I could think about!

ew —I got a mean comment online

 Don't feed the trolls

but shouldn't i stand up 4 myself

 Don't feed the trolls. not worth it.

Hmm. Well, if I couldn't **respond** to this troll, I could still do something creative to show them I didn't care what they thought.*

And it led to a video idea!

If this person thinks my whiskers are basic now, I thought, **I should show them just how basic my whiskers can be!**

The next morning, I created a tutorial called "The Basic Babymouse." It showed my messy whiskers after I rolled out of bed.

It took just a few minutes to create, and I didn't have to get help from Squeak.

I uploaded the video, ran to the bus stop, and forgot all about it. I was too busy catching up on the latest posts from Fabi. She was always posting videos online. I followed her religiously (well, Fabi was a goddess). It was incredible to think that Fabi had once been someone like me—ordinary. Now she was Fabulous.

---

*(Even if I did care what they thought, a lot, and stayed up all night thinking about it.)

THE "BASIC BABYMOUSE"

When I got home from school, the first thing I did was check my new stats. That was when things went from lowercase amazing to uppercase AMAZING!

FABI-LOUS

Things just kept getting better and better. The next morning at school, a couple of girls from my grade ran up to me in the hallway. They were jumping around excitedly. I thought they had to use the bathroom or something, but then I realized they were excited to see **me**.

"How does it feel?" one of the girls asked.

"How does what feel?" I replied. Could

they tell I was wearing two different-colored socks?

"How does it feel to be noticed by **Fabi**?!"

"Huh?"

"You know, Fabi—the famous actress, singer, and dancer?"

"Of course I know her!" I exclaimed. "I've been watching her videos all week. But what does that have to do with **me**?"

Just then, Penny came running down the hall, totally unconcerned with getting a slip from a hall monitor.

"Babymouse!" she squealed. "You'll never believe this! Fabi—yes, **the** Fabi—made a post on social media about how she loves your new look! She even took a picture of herself with twisted whiskers. She calls them twiskers!"

Penny pulled it up on her phone and showed me the proof.

I was too stunned to even think about getting to class on time. Penny gave me a high five and ran off just before the bell sounded. Moments later, the hallway was empty.

Ring!

I didn't move. A hall monitor approached me with a piece of paper.

Oh no, I thought. **I'm going to be in big trouble.**

But when he handed me the paper, instead of being a detention slip, it just said:

Confused, I didn't say anything. I just grabbed my things and hustled to class. What a wacky turn of events!

As soon as I got home that afternoon, I logged on to my computer. My mind was racing with thoughts and questions. Did this mean Fabi and I were friends now?

I kept checking my phone to see if I had any unusual texts or voice mails from numbers I didn't recognize. Usually, I don't pick up the phone if I don't recognize a number, but that day, I was picking up every call. I talked to three robocalls in a row before I turned my spam blocker back on.

How else can I connect with Fabi? I wondered.

I figured getting her attention online had worked once, so maybe it could work again. I reached out to Penny for advice. She always knew what to do.

> How should I get Fabi's attention?

 > Try doing an extra-special tutorial just for her!

Such a great idea!

(Note to self: when famous, hire Penny as your official publicist.)

I decided to tape a new tutorial about the "twiskers."

But what would make it special? I wondered.

I thought about Fabi's songs. She had one called "The Other Way," about going the other way when you felt stuck in a rut. That was perfect!

Basically, I did the exact same look but twisted my whiskers the **other** way.

For Fabi,
someone who
does everything
her own way.

#WhiskerSisters

I uploaded the video and tagged Fabi's username.

Brilliant, I thought. **How could she not love it?**

Now all I had to do was wait. (Well, wait **and** do math homework.)

I wasn't disappointed. The next day, Fabi tagged my video with a heart emoji!

I knew this newfound fame could only mean my life was going to change forever. Everything would be completely different, now that I was friends with a **celebrity**!

GETTING LATTES WITH FABI!

HOLLYWOOD RED CARPETS WITH FABI!

...ACATIONING IN PARIS WITH FABI!

TAKING OUT THE TRASH WITH FABI!

BUT YOU DON'T EVEN LIKE TAKING OUT THE TRASH, BABYMOUSE.

IT'LL BE TOTALLY DIFFERENT WHEN IT'S FAMOUS TRASH!

Sponsor

When I got home from school that day, Mom was sitting in the kitchen, reading mail.

"Welcome home, Babymouse," she said. "How was school?"

"It was awesome!" I replied.

I was going to tell her about the Fabi thing, but my mom wouldn't know who she was. I would have to spend ten minutes explaining the internet to her, when I could be upstairs on my computer, interacting with my many fans.

Luckily, she changed the subject.

"You know, a big package arrived for you," she said.

She pointed to the dining room table, where a brown package sat waiting.

"But I didn't order anything," I replied, confused.

I grabbed a pair of scissors and ripped the package open. I was surprised to see a shiny silver gift bag inside. I slowly opened the bag. It was full of whisker products from Zany! along with a card.

ZANY!

Dear Babymouse,
We love your looks!
Have some ZANY! love on us!
— Your ZANY! friends

Now I was just plain bewildered.

Did they get me mixed up with some-one else? Did I win a contest I didn't even remember entering? Was it a prank by Felicia and her friends, to trick me into putting glue or something nasty on my whiskers?

I brought the package upstairs and carefully inspected it. The products were sealed. Seemed legit.

Next, I looked online to make sure all the items in the bag were real Zany! products. They were, as far as I could tell.

Lastly, I made sure the return address matched the company headquarters. It checked out, so I decided to have some fun playing around with the products. You might say I had a Zany! time.

☆ ♡ ☆

I assumed the Zany! mailing was a fluke, but when I got home from school the next day, it happened again. On my doorstep were even more packages, from whisker-styling companies all over the country!

I could barely get into the house, there were so many boxes in the way.

I opened the boxes to discover all the top whisker products! There was whisker shampoo, conditioner, serum, mousse, mask, defrizzer, gel, and spray. They even included a whisker cap, which I learned is like a shower cap to keep your whiskers from getting wet.

I still didn't understand why anyone would send me all these #freebies, but it was certainly something I could get used to.

I hoped Penny would be able to shed some light on the situation. When I saw her at school the next day, I told her what had happened. But instead of being worried, she was excited.

"Babymouse! These companies want to sponsor you!" she explained.

"Sponsor me?" I asked. I had never heard of that.

"They want you to use their products and talk about them in your tutorials!" she continued.

"Okay," I replied slowly. "I guess I can do that."

It didn't seem like a bad trade-off to get lots of free stuff in exchange for a little publicity. So when I got home from school that afternoon, I began to try out the products.

Some were for straightening.

Others were for curling.

One was a highlighting dye.

In a perfect world, I would have been patient and tried them one at a time. I would also have remembered which one was which, and what product did what. But in the end, I was so excited that I kind of used everything all at once.

I had heard of all the products except one. There was a neon-orange tube of something called WHIZZZZKER. The label just said, "Guaranteed to give your whiskers that certain something."

WHIZZZZKER

Guaranteed to give your whiskers that certain something

I didn't know what a "certain something" was, but it sounded better than an uncertain nothing. I decided to give it a try. What did I have to lose, right?

As it turned out, the answer was . . . all my whiskers!

HUH, TALK ABOUT A
CERTAIN SOMETHING.

TYPICAL.

DM!

osing my whiskers was a major set-back. How could I be the whisker wizard without my iconic Twist? If Fabi found out, would she drop me as a friend and follower?

I needed Penny's advice.

u around?

 yah. video chat?

Can't.

 ??

I burned my whiskers off! I can't show my face to the world!

oh no! but u can at least show me!

I can't show ANYONE!

Babymouse, don't u think u r overreacting just a *little* bit?

ME?! OVERREACTING?!

Lol they're whiskers! They'll grow back!

It was obvious Penny didn't understand the seriousness of the situation. But what did I expect? She couldn't possibly understand the pressure I was under. It looked like I was on my own.

I searched my box of whisker goodies to see what I could do to fix my face.

I stumbled across Whisker-Grow, a product from yet another #sponsor. It would supposedly make my whiskers grow back "20x" faster!

After reading the instructions, I applied Whisker-Grow to my bare skin.

Better not use too much, I thought. **Don't want to end up tripping over my own whiskers!**

But the next morning, my whiskers still looked exactly the same!

Really, 20x faster? I thought. **More like 20x slower! Talk about false advertising.**

But I had no time to think about it, because I would be late for school. Luckily, I found whisker extensions in my product box! (Thanks, #sponsors!) They would be handy for hiding my missing whiskers.

☆ ♡ ☆

After I used Whisker-Grow and whisker extensions for a week, my whiskers grew back and my life returned to normal. Well, I guess "normal" isn't the right word, because I was still really popular at school—and that was anything **but** normal.

Anyway, in the midst of my popularity spike, someone new sent me a message.

WHISKER MAESTRO

Love your Twist, Babymouse!

I didn't want to just start talking to a random stranger—that could be dangerous!—so I looked up the Whisker Maestro online. I had gotten pretty good at looking things up on the internet. So in no time, I knew everything about this person.

His name was Nicky. He wore a ton of makeup. He had an outlandish hairstyle (possibly a wig). But most importantly, he had fabulous whiskers.

Nicky was what they called a whisker influencer. As the Whisker Maestro, his signature look was whiskers shaped like a musical note.

I was flattered that he had reached out to me. I thought a little about it, and then decided to reply.

Nicky messaged me back, and we continued texting. Soon, it was almost as if we were online friends. He even gave me advice on how to become an influencer like him! He told me what sites to go on, which kinds of posts got the most engagement, and so on.

WM Definitely avoid
WHIZZZZKER!
It melts off your
whiskers.

Yeah, I found out
the hard way.

WM Me too.

Nicky and I were always laughing. It really felt like the beginning of a beautiful friendship.

#OperationBesties

I didn't feel like I was on my own anymore, now that I was friends with Nicky. It was great to have someone new to bond with. My regular friends at school, especially Wilson, didn't really understand what I was going through now that I was #sponsored.

There was so much pressure. The sponsors were counting on me, and I didn't want to let them down.

Nicky and I could commiserate about the pressure of constantly creating new looks and filming tutorials. He even told me his little sister had filmed his videos, just like Squeak did for me! We were two peas in a pod.

Meanwhile, I was still busy trying all the new products that came to my house. So many packages were arriving every day that I wasn't reading the mailing labels anymore. I just assumed they were all for me, all the time.

This was fine until I almost put Sea-Monkey eggs from my little brother's science kit onto my whiskers.

Gross!

But it did give me an idea: if I could get Squeak to help me test the products, I could do **twice** as many tutorials in the same amount of time.

And he was more than willing to participate . . . even though he didn't have any whiskers.

Nicky offered to help me out by liking my looks and using the same products. It was a whisker win-win situation! I decided to call our partnership #OperationBesties.

Nicky and I started to work together online. We reviewed, recommended, and swapped products. Sometimes, we would just chat online for hours about absolutely nothing.

I got a message from Nicky:

WM Let's do a tutorial together!

IRL?

WM Nah, by video.

how does that work?

WM We can use a split screen!

kewl! let's do it.

The idea of a split screen sounded awe-some! I pictured our video covered with bananas, whipped cream, gooey choco-late fudge, strawberry sauce, and a cherry on top.

But when I looked it up online, I learned that a split screen was just two videos put next to each other. Oh well.

Working together was fun, though. It was a lot easier to talk with someone else during

a video than to do everything myself. Plus,
Nicky had lots of cool technical skills, and
could add filters and other special effects to
our videos.

Sometimes, it seemed weird that I had never **met** Nicky in real life. It was kind of unusual having a virtual-only relationship. But he and I worked so well together that I started to wonder if all my friendships should be virtual ones.

The collaboration with Nicky seemed to be paying off. My subscribers and followers were still growing, and the likes and comments were ticking up on each of my videos.

Just when I thought that things couldn't get any better, I got a new alert:

ALERT CENTER

WW WHISKER WIZARDS 6m ago

ALERT:
Fabi: Babymouse + Whisker Maestro = World Peace

I was totally **blown away.** My idol, Fabi, had created a post about me! This was more than a heart emoji. It was a post specifically mentioning me by name!

I immediately texted Nicky to tell him the good news. But just as my text went out, I got one from him.

WM OMG! Did u see Fabi's post?

omg! did you c fabi's post?

WM lol #greatminds

haha 🙂

CAN YOU SEE ME ROLLING MY VIRTUAL EYES, BABYMOUSE?

Whispers

 OperationBesties was a total success! I felt like I was floating on air. Or sitting on top of the world. Or floating on top of the world. Or any number of the million other things people say when everything seems too good to be true.

Nicky and I worked perfectly together. It was as if we had a Vulcan Mind-Meld. Or maybe a Whisker Mind-Meld.

When I got to school the following Monday, something felt different. As I walked down the hallways, the other girls started to look at me funny, giving me a weird side-eye. No one ran up to me to talk about my latest look or ask for advice on how to do their whiskers. No one even acknowledged me at all (except, you know, my **regular** friends like Penny and Wilson).

Instead, people started whispering when they saw me coming.

I made a mental checklist of all the reasons why people could be talking about me.

1. Did I have something in my teeth?

But no, nothing was different. Or at least, nothing about **me** was different.

I took a look around. I couldn't help but notice that more and more girls were doing their whiskers in a "note" instead of a Twist. The Whisker Maestro's signature style!

At first, I didn't think anything of it, but I was a little bummed that my look wasn't the most popular anymore.

I tried to put it out of my head, but the musical note was taking over.

Even on the lunch lady!

☆ ♡ ☆

Things got even worse when I got home from school. There wasn't a huge pile of products from potential sponsors. In fact, there was only one box, and it was from WHIZZZZKERS. What on earth was going on?!

I ran upstairs with the package and dumped it on the bathroom counter. No way was I going to burn my whiskers off using that junk again.

I'll just go online and see my fans and feel the love, I thought. **Then everything will be just fine.**

But things didn't get any better when I logged on to my computer.

I went to the Whisker Wizards website and saw I had **lost** some subscribers. I was shocked and confused.

☆ ♡ ☆

The next day at school, I was in the bathroom when I overheard some girls from my grade gossiping. I was in a stall, so they couldn't see me.

At first, they were talking about teachers and homework and stuff, but then the conversation changed and they started talking about **me**!

Could it be true?! I thought, shocked. **Is the Whisker Maestro really telling everyone I used mayonnaise on my whiskers?!**

First of all, I thought Nicky and I were **friends.** Why would he do anything to hurt me or my reputation? Sheesh! So much for #OperationBesties!

Second of all, it wasn't even true! I used horseradish for my signature look, not mayonnaise.

Third of all, what did it matter to anyone what I used on my whiskers?! They had loved my new look last week!

I waited until their voices were gone, and then I flushed the toilet and went to wash my hands. As I looked at my face in the mirror, I noticed that my eyes looked puffy and my cheeks were pink from embarrassment.

What did I do? What **could** I do?

My twisted whiskers stared back at me, almost taunting me.

I wondered if I should be changing my Twist look to a musical note, too. I wanted to be cool and on trend, but I didn't want to betray my own style just to fit in. And what did it even matter? If people were avoiding me because they thought I used mayonnaise on my whiskers, they were going to avoid me whether I had a Twist **or** a note style.

I was floored. Literally! I sat on the floor to think about everything that had just happened. I wanted to go home and hide under the covers forever. But there was still a whole day of school left. **Ugh.**

I took a deep breath and exited the bathroom.

SMACK!

I ran right into the hall monitor. At first, I was relieved to see it was the same hall monitor from the week before. I knew he was a fan.

But he handed me a detention slip—
a real one—so I guess it didn't matter.

Tea Is Spilled

I didn't understand what had happened. I hadn't done anything wrong, and suddenly everyone had turned against me! It was all so confusing, and my feelings were more than a little hurt.

Desperate, I turned to Penny for advice.

"Babymouse, you have to spill the tea," she told me.

Spill tea? I hadn't spilled anything since I was in kindergarten. (At least not on purpose.)

Penny assured me that it didn't matter what had **actually** happened. She said that with celebrity feuds, people only care about "juicy drama." She convinced me to make a video telling my "side" of the story.

I didn't have any better ideas, so I wrote a script and practiced reading it over and over. And let me tell you, it didn't matter how many times I practiced. As soon as the camera started rolling, I got tongue-tied like it was the first video I'd ever made.

It ended up like this:

● REC

HI. I'M BABYMOUSE. AS MANY OF YOU KNOW, MY NAME IS BABYMOUSE.

WELL, ANYWAY, I'M MAKING THIS VIDEO TODAY BECAUSE THIS PERSON WHO I THOUGHT WAS MY FRIEND, WHISKER MAESTRO, BUT IS ACTUALLY NOT MY FRIEND, WHISKER MAESTRO, STARTED A RUMOR ABOUT ME USING MAYONNAISE ON MY WHISKERS.

THE ACTUAL RUMOR IS THAT I USE MAYONNAISE ON MY WHISKERS. OKAY, BUT HERE'S THE THING. I DIDN'T—AND I DON'T—USE MAYONNAISE ON MY WHISKERS!
TO BE HONEST, I DON'T EVEN LIKE MAYONNAISE ON MY SANDWICHES! WELL, ACTUALLY, THAT'S NOT TRUE. BECAUSE I EAT IT MIXED IN WITH TUNA FISH AND CHICKEN SALAD, AND SOMETIMES EVEN EGG SALAD, THOUGH I DON'T REALLY LIKE EGG SALAD ALL THAT MUCH.
BUT ANYWAY, WHAT I'M TRYING TO SAY IS THAT I DON'T USE MAYONNAISE ON MY WHISKERS. OKAY, THAT'S IT. THANKS FOR LISTENING.
HOW'D I DO?
I DON'T THINK I'VE EVER HEARD ANYONE TALK ABOUT MAYONNAISE SO MUCH. IT'S MADE ME A BIT HUNGRY, I CONFESS.

I took a deep breath, uploaded the video, and refreshed the page. I was hoping that would be the end of it. I was wrong.

Almost immediately, people started sending me comments and DMs that said my statement was offensive to people who **did** like to use mayonnaise on their whiskers.

WHAT?! I thought. I couldn't win!

I had no problem with people using mayonnaise on their whiskers—I was just trying to say I don't use mayonnaise on **my** whiskers!

Ugh, I thought. **What a headache!**

There was nothing for me to do but record another video, explaining myself yet again.

HI, THIS IS BABYMOUSE AGAIN.

● REC

SOME OF YOU HAVE BEEN MESSAGING ME TO SAY YOU LIKE TO USE MAYONNAISE ON YOUR WHISKERS, AND YOU FELT MY VIDEO SUGGESTED I DON'T APPROVE OF YOUR USING MAYONNAISE ON YOUR WHISKERS.
I'M JUST RECORDING THIS VIDEO TO SAY I FULLY APPROVE OF USING MAYONNAISE ON YOUR WHISKERS, BUT I PERSONALLY DO NOT USE MAYONNAISE ON MINE.
SO BASICALLY, TO RECAP, MY NAME IS BABYMOUSE, AND I SUPPORT ANYONE WHO DOES USE MAYONNAISE ON THEIR WHISKERS, BECAUSE IT'S A FREE COUNTRY AND EVERYONE SHOULD BE ABLE TO USE WHATEVER THEY WANT ON THEIR WHISKERS, WITHOUT OTHER PEOPLE TELLING THEM THEY CAN'T. AND, REALLY, IT'S NO ONE'S BUSINESS WHAT ANOTHER PERSON USES ON THEIR WHISKERS ANYWAY.
SO, YEAH. THAT'S IT, AGAIN. THANKS. BYE.
REC

☆ ♥ ☆

I was hoping this video would really be the end of it. But instead, it looked like I had just opened the floodgates on a debate about people using mayonnaise on their whiskers. Supporters started posting #TeamMayo, and haters started posting #HoldTheMayo. Then a new group of people started posting #MayoTheForceBeWithYou.

In no time, #MayoGate had taken over the whole site!

The Whisker Maestro didn't hesitate to jump into the conversation. I guess I should have seen it coming. He even stooped so low as to take a clip from the original video, of me saying "The actual rumor is that I use mayonnaise on my whiskers," and cut it down to just "I use mayonnaise on my whiskers."

He posted the clip with the caption "Babymouse admits to using mayonnaise on her whiskers!"

I couldn't believe it. He totally took what I said out of context—on purpose! Some friend he was turning out to be. . . .

I tried to stop the drama by posting, "Look! I really don't care **at all** about #Mayo!" But in my rush to post, I accidentally left a typo, so it read:

Whisker Wizards

babymouse_actual

Look! I really don't care at all about #May!

Then a whole group of people with birthdays in May started sending me nasty messages.

(Weirdly, I got a handful of support for my alleged hatred of May. Go figure.)

This was spiraling completely out of control! Everything I did was only fanning the flames and making things worse. I decided, as hard as it was, to just stop posting and hope the thing would die down on its own.

Unfortunately, it didn't. A bunch of the companies that sponsored me immediately

---

(W) WHIZZZZKER

Disclaimer:

Sponsored content does not necessarily reflect the views or opinions of our organization as a whole. For information about our company values, please see our About page, which contains our official mission statement. For more information or media queries, please contact PublicRelations@Whizzzzkers.com.

(Leave us out of this.)

♡ ⃝ ⤴

issued statements about the mayo controversy. I watched as they popped up, one by
one, on my feed.

Le sigh.

☆ ♡ ☆

The next day at school, I kept my head
down. I didn't raise my hand. I didn't talk to
anyone. Above all, I avoided every possible
thing related to mayonnaise.

Of course, the lunch lady served me a
giant egg salad sandwich.

Show the Receipts

I was starting to wish I had never gone viral. All I wanted was to be normal again, to be myself without everyone telling me what to do or how to think.

But it was too late for me. The Whisker Maestro seemed to be loving the drama. He kept posting things about our "beef" to keep the controversy going.

That's when things started going from bad to really, really bad.

The Whisker Maestro—I was using his online persona name, now that we were no longer friends—began to release snippets from our conversations as "proof of mayo use."

He even posted the link to the original recipe I used, which had mayonnaise as an ingredient.

GBB - Make your own natural whisker serum

HOUSEHOLD INGREDIENTS!

20% OFF MAYO

MAYO!

CLICK HERE

INGREDIENTS:
Lemon, mustard, vinegar, mayonnaise

WARNING: PARENTAL GUIDANCE RECOMMENDED

Recipe Copyright © Mayo Council International

DIRECTIONS:

1. Begin with mayonnaise. Lots and lots of creamy, delicious mayonnaise. Stir in the remaining ingredients.

2. Apply to face. Or whiskers. Whatever.

3. Wait. Maybe 10 minutes? Who knows. This

"The whole thing is ridiculous," I told Penny on the bus home after school.

"Listen, Babymouse," she said. "This looks really bad. From now on, you need to do everything I tell you."

My brain was so fried that I just agreed.

"Okay, what do I do?"

"First things first," she told me. "We need to show your receipts!"

I looked into my bag and pulled out all the receipts I could find.

Penny laughed and shook her head.

"Not those kinds of receipts, Baby-

CORNER PHARMACY

24-Pack of Perfectly Peppermint Gum	$9.99
	$9.99
SUBTOTAL	$0.80
TAX	$10.79
TOTAL	$11.00
CASH	$0.21
CHANGE	

Monster Movie Fest E-ticket

TOTAL: $17.45

mouse," she said. "Receipts are proof of your side of the story."

"Oh!" I replied, finally getting it.

Penny seemed to know exactly what to do. I decided to just give her control of my Whisker Wizards account. If she couldn't rein the chaos in, no one could.

Once I got home, I sent her my login information and tried to focus on other things while she got to work. She said it should take about an hour.

```
         SCHOOL CAFETERIA


Egg Salad Sandwich:     $4.95
Extra Mayo:             $0.30


                        $5.25
  TOTAL:
```

One hour. That wasn't so bad. Surely, I could come up with enough things to do that weren't based on social media. I'd already finished my homework during study period.

I sat on my bed, and my mind went blank. I tried to think about what I used to do before I became an online celebrity, but I couldn't think of anything. It seemed like such a long time ago.

Did I like to do jigsaw puzzles? I tried to remember.

Judging by the age range of the only puzzle I could find, I think maybe I didn't.

How about coloring? I asked myself.

But my coloring book was covered in dust, and all the pages were already filled in.

badymouse

ace!

Squids live under the sea. Would you?

Maybe I can watch kids' shows with Squeak?

I went downstairs and plopped on the couch beside him. I started to watch, but the show was so nonsensical and the music was so cheesy that it started driving me insane. Surely, anything—really, **anything** at all— had to be better than watching that garbage.

Garbage! That gave me an idea.

I tracked down my mom to see if she had any chores for me to do.

"Mom, is there any cleaning around the house I can help out with?" I asked.

"What?" Mom replied with an eyebrow raised. "Who are you, and what did you do with the real Babymouse?"

She was so worried that she made me go upstairs and take my temperature.

Thermometer in mouth, I broke down and texted Penny. It had only been sixteen minutes.

I was back to trying other hobbies. But nothing was working out so well.

When I tried to meditate, my mind just drifted off to the online feud.

When I opened my diary, I started writing about the Whisker Maestro.

I called Wilson to chat, but it turned into me unloading on him about everything that had happened.

AND **THEN** HE TOLD EVERYONE I ACTUALLY **LIKED** MAYONNAISE. CAN YOU BELIEVE THAT? ME, LIKING MAYONNAISE! PREPOSTEROUS!

BLEEP

BOOP

UH-HUH, YEAH, BABYMOUSE. LISTEN, I HAVE TO GO.

I collapsed on my bed and took a nap.

Ding!

I was woken up about forty-five minutes later by a soft noise. I wiped the drool from my mouth and checked my phone. Penny had texted me.

Well, I have some good news and some bad news.

ok! wut is it?

which do u want 2 hear first

ummm start with the bad news

the bad news is there is not *actually* any good news

Penny told me she went through all the DMs between me and the Whisker Maestro, and there wasn't anything that could help my case. If I posted any of my messages, they would only show I'd misspelled a lot of words.

~~Tipical.~~

Typical.

She told me that things online had pretty much stayed the same, except a new poll had popped up on Whisker Wizards.

WHAT TEAM ARE YOU ON? VOTE NOW!

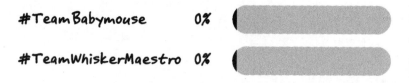

#TeamBabymouse   0%

#TeamWhiskerMaestro 0%

I couldn't believe it! An online **poll**? How humiliating. I tried to tell myself that maybe my fans would come out in big numbers to support me. Surely, some people who had fawned all over me just days before would still be on my side, no? How much damage could the mayo rumors do to my overall reputation, right? **Right?**

☆ ♡ ☆

The next day at school, I got a rude awakening. I witnessed the debate in real life as I walked down the hallway.

DRAMA-RAMA

The next morning, my fears were confirmed: the Whisker Maestro had completely swept the online poll.

WHAT TEAM ARE YOU ON? VOTE NOW!

#TeamBabymouse   0.25%

#TeamWhiskerMaestro 99.75%

There must have been some mistake! Was there really **that** big of a landslide?

At school, Penny came right over to my locker. She gave me a hug, which is how I knew things were **really** bad.

"Don't forget," she said. "There could be a huge margin of error with that kind of poll."

"Yeah!" said Felicia, walking by. "In reality, the Whisker Maestro could have won the whole thing!"

HA!

Argh!

"Anyway," Penny said, ignoring her, "I voted for you, so I know that can't possibly be true."

I didn't have the guts to tell her I also voted for myself—fourteen times.

After school, I half-heartedly tried to do some new whisker looks, but nothing was quite working. I had also run out of free products, now that the sponsorships had dried up.

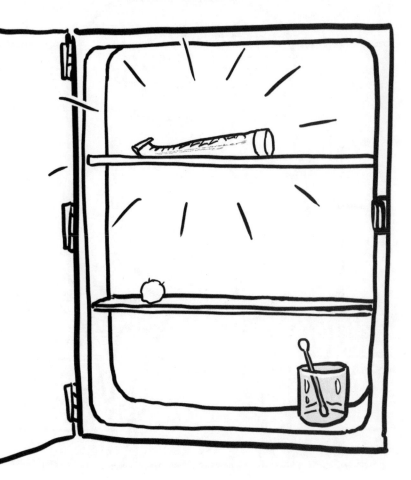

I guess I should have rationed things better, because after I'd used up my products, I moved on to Dad's whisker mousse. I went through the whole bottle, and he was forced to use the only thing left in the bathroom . . . Whizzzzkers.

I decided to walk to the pharmacy to get some more whisker products, for old times' sake. I couldn't believe I had to buy products for my whiskers.

How the mighty have fallen, I thought with a sigh.

What?! The Whisker Maestro was at the same pharmacy as me! I was sure it was him, even though he wasn't wearing makeup, a wig (it **was** a wig—I knew it!), or whisker extensions. Without all the add-ons, he looked, well, **normal.**

I stared at him for a long time. Then I took out my phone and snapped a picture of him on the sly.

Maybe I could post the picture of Nicky without his fake facade to show everyone who he really is, I thought.

His fans would be shocked to know the #truth. And they, like me, would be horrified to learn he was buying **Basic Whiskers**! That was the most **boring** whisker product out there. If only his sponsors knew! The truth could destroy him.

Suddenly, I felt like I had all the power back. With just one simple post, I could blow up his sponsorships, shock all his fans, and maybe even make myself relevant again!

Sure, Nicky had never **said** he didn't wear makeup, a wig, or whisker extensions. But just the same, celebrity followers never like being deceived.

And it would feel so good to have everyone on my side again. . . .

But then what? I wondered.

Then he would fall from fame and be in the same position as me? Then he would feel as terrible as I did? I didn't really want that, either. I wasn't going to stoop to that level just to be popular.

You're better than that, Babymouse, I reminded myself.

I took a deep breath and deleted the photo. Fame wasn't worth being **mean** for.

But I still wanted answers. I thought about whether to go over and confront him directly. It was hard to believe that this would be our first meeting in person.

What's the worst that could happen?

I wondered. **He could be rude to my face, and somehow use the interaction to make me even LESS popular?**

I didn't think that was possible.

Nicky still hadn't noticed me, and I made sure to keep it that way.

Just when I had mustered up enough courage to talk to him, I tripped over my own feet and knocked into a giant display of denture cream.

CRASH!

The whole display fell onto the floor around me.

Nicky rushed over to see what had happened, along with an angry manager.

"Are you okay, ma'am?" the manager asked. It was pretty clear he did not actually care whether I was okay.

I could feel my face blushing dark red as I stammered, "Well, um—yeah, yeah, I'm o-o-okay."

He nodded and picked up his walkie-talkie.

"Cleanup on aisle seven, please. Cleanup on aisle seven."

Two employees arrived to clean up aisle seven.

Nicky had just spotted me. "Baby-mouse?" he asked, looking into my face. "Is that . . . is that **you**?"

"Yep," I responded coolly. "I'm surprised you'd even recognize me outside the mayonnaise section."

Instead of saying something snarky back, he burst out laughing.

"Good one," he said, bending down to help pick up the mess. "Are you sure you're okay?"

"Like you care," I huffed.

I didn't understand why he was acting like everything was fine between us. Everything was **not** fine, and I wasn't going to pretend it was.

"I do care, actually," Nicky replied, caught off guard. "We're friends, Babymouse!"

"Friends?!" I snapped. "How can you think we're still friends?"

"What?" he asked. "Are you still mad about the mayonnaise thing?"

THE MAYONNAISE THING? I wanted to scream. He made it sound like I was over-reacting to a small mistake instead of dealing with a major life event that led to the fall of my whisker dynasty!

"I'll have you know **THE MAYONNAISE THING** was one of the worst things to ever happen to me in my whole, entire life!" I erupted.

Nicky started laughing.

"I'm sorry to laugh," he said between gasps. "But you're so funny. No wonder everyone loves you."

"Huh?" Flattery was not going to work on this mouse. Not no way, not no how.

"Look," he went on. "The mayonnaise thing wasn't real. I mean it was, but not in real life. It was just to get clicks. Everyone loves drama!"

"Are you serious?" I asked. "So it was all made up?"

"Of course," Nicky said, looking confused. "You thought it was real?"

I nodded. Of course I thought it was real!

"Not at all," Nicky continued. "See, a lot of influencers get into phony feuds to drive more clicks. I thought you knew that. It happens all the time online."

Hmph.

"Well, you should have told me at the beginning. Not to mention all the kids at my school. I had no idea. My life has been a nightmare because of the fallout online. And that poll—yikes!"

"Oh, whoops," Nicky replied. "That was my fault, too. I used an algorithm to get a bunch of wizard bots to vote for me. They voted thousands of times."

Wizard bots?

If his wizard bots voted for him thousands of times, that means A LOT of people voted for ME, I thought.

This whole thing was getting weirder and weirder. My head was starting to hurt.

"Look, Babymouse," Nicky said. "I'm really sorry for hurting you. I guess I didn't think about how it would seem to you IRL. I won't do anything like that again—without letting you know and making sure you want to play along."

"Okay," I replied. "That sounds like a good start."

"I do hope we can still be friends," he said. "Just maybe not online."

He put out his hand to shake.

I was still unsure, but he seemed sincere in his apology.

I looked at his hand for a minute without shaking it. I would give him another chance.

(I secretly thought how glad I was that I didn't post my picture of him!)

I decided to change the subject.

"So, what's that you got there?" I asked, pointing to the Basic Whiskers bottle in his basket.

"This stuff is the best!" he said. "My mom uses it. It's actually one of my favorite products."

"That's funny," I replied. "My mom uses it, too. So do I, sometimes."

"Along with denture cream?" Nicky pointed to my basket, which had a couple of tubes that had fallen off the display.

"Don't you dare think of starting that rumor," I warned.

He shook his head innocently, and we both laughed. Now that I realized the feud was all fake, I felt a lot better.

Because there was so much to talk about, and it was our first time meeting in person, we decided to go grab sandwiches at the diner next door.

We laughed as we enjoyed our sandwiches. We got along in person just as well as we did online (you know, before the feud).

Suddenly, a camera flashed outside the window. Someone took a picture of us covered in mustard!

No Comment

inally, I had made it to the weekend. Outside my window, the sun was shining. Birds were chirping. My neighbor was mowing her lawn. It was the start of a beautiful day, and I was enjoying it from the comfort of my own bed.

Just then, my phone rang. It was Penny.

"Hello," I said groggily.

"Did you see it?" she asked.

"See what?!" I asked. I wished people

would assume I had no idea what they were talking about early in the morning. . . .

"Hold on," she said. "I'm texting you the link right now."

. . . whisker whispers . . .

SCANDAL ROCKS THE WHISKER-NET!

RIVALS BABYMOUSE AND MAESTRO SPOTTED EATING SANDWICHES TOGETHER

WHISKER MAESTRO:
"No comment!"

BABYMOUSE:
"No comment!"

MUSTARD-COATED WHISKERS!

One of our eagle-eyed whisker whisperers spotted online rivals BABYMOUSE and WHISKER MAESTRO grabbing lunch together at a neighborhood eatery. Why were these two together? And what was in their whiskers? MUSTARD! #MayoGate may be over, but #MustardGate has just begun!

"Seriously?!" I groaned "What a nightmare!"

"I know," she said. "It's the same thing all over again."

Glued to my computer, I watched my latest scandal unfold across the internet. Images and posts popped up on my screen.

"When did it become such a terrible thing to use condiments?!" I asked. "Am I just supposed to eat everything dry for the rest of my life?"

"You know, that's actually not a bad idea," she said. "We should do damage control ASAP. Maybe you could issue a statement about..."

As she rambled on, I started to zone out. I looked out my window.

The sky was blue, and there were birds flying. They seemed so free and happy. They didn't have to worry about social media or mayonnaise or whiskers.

"You know what, Penny?" I said, interrupting her. "I think I'm going to take a break from social media."

"Really?" she asked. "I didn't even know that was possible."

"I think so, yeah," I said. "I'm going to live in the real world for a while."

"Okay," Penny said. "But you know where to find me if you need me."

"I do," I replied. "And I appreciate you always being there for me. Thank you."

"That's what friends are for!"

After we hung up, I stared at my computer.

When did social media become stressful instead of fun? I wondered.

I thought about this for a moment, and then <GASP> deleted all my accounts.

I thought it would be easy, but it turns out that nothing is easy when it comes to social media.

Looking at the empty screen, I expected
to feel anxious, but instead I just felt **free**!

I looked at my computer screen and searched for maps of things to do in my neighborhood. Of course, I immediately got sucked into a beauty site about trending nail polish looks.

WANT TO BE A "WHISKER WIZARD"?

GRAB A FEW KITCHEN INGREDIENTS AND LET'S GET STARTED!

FOR "BRIGHTER" WHISKERS, TRY A FEW SQUEEZES OF FRESH LEMON JUICE AND THEN GO SIT IN THE SUN.

MAYONNAISE STRENGTHENS YOUR WHISKERS!

WANT TO TAME THE FRIZZIES?
DAB ON A LITTLE OLIVE OIL!

AVOCADO IS A GREAT MOISTURIZER!

☆ ♡ ☆

About the Authors

Jennifer L. Holm and **Matthew Holm** are a **New York Times** bestselling sister-and-brother team. They are the creators behind several popular series: Babymouse, Squish, The Evil Princess vs. the Brave Knight, and My First Comics. The Eisner Award–winning Babymouse books have introduced millions of children to graphic novels. Jennifer is also the **New York Times** bestselling author of **The Four-teenth Goldfish** and several other highly acclaimed novels, including three Newbery Honor winners: **Our Only May Amelia, Penny from Heaven,** and **Turtle in Para-dise.** Matthew is also the author of **Marvin and the Moths** with Jonathan Follett.

BABYMOUSE
TALES FROM THE LOCKER

New York Times bestselling authors of *Sunny Side Up*
JENNIFER L. HOLM & MATTHEW HOLM

School-Tripped

Will a class field trip with **no chaperones** be as thrilling as Babymouse thinks? Or will life in the Big City trip her up big-time?

BABYMOUSE
TALES FROM THE LOCKER

New York Times bestselling authors of *Sunny Side Up*
JENNIFER L. HOLM & MATTHEW HOLM

Curtain Call

Will Babymouse's performance be a showstopper . . . or should someone actually try to stop her?